The Pirates of Plagiarism

RAAWK!

Kathleen Fox and Lisa Downey

Illustrations by Lisa Downey

UpstartBooks

Madison, Wisconsin

www.upstartbooks.com

Outside the Clearview School Library, trouble was lurking.

"Thar she sits, mateys," whispered Captain Bumbo. "That treasure is ours for the takin'."

"But Captain Bumbo," said Mizzy. "What about the lass in the corner?"

"I think she's what's called the librarian, sir," said Fluke. "Heard their kind are tougher than Blackbeard and Captain Kidd combined."

Starbird the parrot squawked, "Smarter, too—RAAWK!—smarter, too!"

"Hush up that parrot, Fluke!" Captain Bumbo hissed. "You're all wimpy landlubbers! We're goin' in, and no stinkin' li-berry-an is gonna stop us. Follow me!"

The crew slipped inside. Grabbing library loot along the way, the pirates crept to where Mrs. Finch, the librarian, was shelving books.

"Where's the key to unlock the treasure chest?" demanded the captain.

"Key? There is no key. It's just a display," said Mrs. Finch.

Captain Bumbo looked puzzled and turned to his crew. "Aargh, she's tryin' to fool us, mates!" He moved closer to Mrs. Finch. "This is your last chance, liberry lady. Give us the treasure chest key!"

"I told you, there's no key to that—"

Bumbo cut the librarian off. "So you want to play it that way, aye?" He pointed to his pirate gang. "Mizzy and Tug, capture her! Fluke and Copycat—to the treasure chest!"

"No treasure—RAAWK!—no treasure."

Captain Bumbo's face turned a peculiar shade of purple. "Fluke, get that loony-bagoony bird away from me or I'll make him into soup!"

"Did someone say soup?" Copycat's stomach started to grumble. "I've never tried parrot soup. Do we have sea biscuits to go with that?"

As the pirates eagerly circled the treasure chest, they heard soft footsteps. Mizzy turned around. "Uh-oh, Captain. We've got children on our backs." "What?" sputtered the captain. "We can't fight no cocka-dimmy children!"

"I'd rather be eaten alive by a giant squid than cross swords with them small fries," Tug whimpered.

"Kids are scarier than sea boat scurvy!" Fluke quivered.

"Stay calm, mates," the captain instructed. "Leave 'em to me."

The children wandered over to the pirates. "Excuse me, where's Mrs. Finch?" a boy asked.

The captain grinned slyly. "She's tied up at the moment."

"So, can you help us finish our reports?" asked a girl.

The pirates looked blankly at each other.

"Reports?" asked the captain.

"Our reports on sharks," she replied.

"Sharks? Well, I—Captain Q. Bumbo, III—once wrestled me a hammerhead." The captain lifted his shirt. "Got a scar here to prove it."

"That looks like a silly tattoo," giggled a girl in the back.

"Smarty pants," grumbled Bumbo under his breath.

Another girl raised her hand. "Excuse me, Mr. Bumbo, we need to do research on the computer."

"Of course you do!" bluffed the captain. "Ahem . . . lead the way." The pirates followed the children uneasily toward the computers.

"Mrs. Finch told us to read about sharks," said the girl. "Then put what we read into our own words, and say where we got the information."

"Read!" cried the captain. "Why waste time readin' when you can just take them words and put 'em right smack into your report?"

"*Because*," another girl explained, "That's just cutting and pasting."

"Don't cut and paste—RAAWK!—don't cut and paste!" sang Starbird.

"Call it what you will," said Captain Bumbo, swatting at the parrot.

"But that's plagiarism!" the children cried.

"Of course it is!" shouted Captain Bumbo. He turned and whispered to Fluke, "You can read—go find out what that 'play-jer-izmo' word means, and take that feather-brained bird with you."

Just then, one of the boys approached carrying a thick book. "I need a drawing of a shark for my report cover."

"Well, then," declared Tug. "Here's the solution." He swung his cutlass at an open page, and a photograph dropped to the floor. "Presto, a shark picture for your report!"

The children stared at Tug in disbelief. "You're in TROU—ble!" they chorused.

"Trouble, mates, is me middle name," Tug boasted.

"I thought it was Francis," purred Copycat.

Tug shot Copycat a look that could sink a ship.

"Why didn't you just copy the shark picture on the scanner?" asked the boy.

"Did you say 'copy'?" Copycat leapt forward, grabbed his quill, and with a few quick strokes, copied an entire page from the book.

The cat handed the page to the boy and said, "I can copy anything word-for-word. And trace anything, too. See?"

A girl stepped forward. "I'm pretty sure you're not supposed to copy stuff word-for-word. Mrs. Finch says you have to tell where you got the information, whether you trace it or copy it."

"Not word-for-word—RAAWK!—not word-for-word!" squawked Starbird from the reference section.

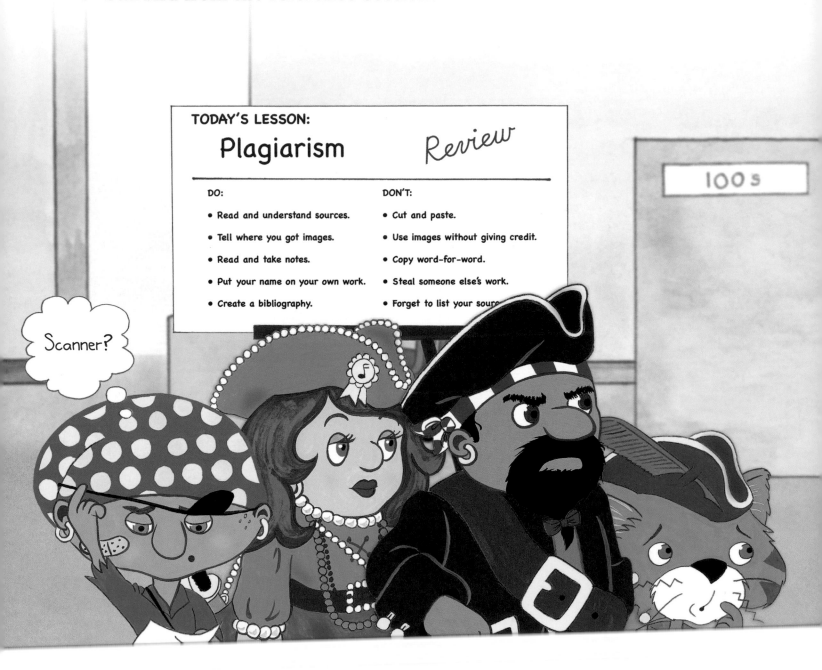

"Well, do you see your sweet little Mrs. Finch here?" Captain Bumbo sneered. A muffled cry came from the back of the library. The pirates' eyes widened. "Heh-heh," the captain laughed. "That parrot is always making crazy noises."

The children looked confused. Everything the pirates had said was exactly what Mrs. Finch had taught them NOT to do.

The other boy heaved a big sigh and said, "At this rate, I'm never going to finish my report on time!"

Captain Bumbo spied a neat blue folder and held it up. "What is this?" he demanded.

"It's my report on sharks," said a girl proudly.

"Is that so, me little barnacle? And it's finished—lock, stock, and barrel, aye?"

The girl nodded, smiling.

The captain tapped the boy standing next to him. "Here mate, just plunder this report from the lass. Shuffle a word or two and put your name right on it—report finished."

The girl's smile faded. The boy narrowed his eyes and stared hard at the pirate, then said slowly:

"*That's* something only a *swab* would do."

The pirates gasped and the captain's mouth dropped wide open. He'd never been called the lowest insult to any pirate before. For the first time, Captain Bumbo felt a little nervous.

"Are you sure you don't know where our librarian is?" asked the boy, eyeing thc captain suspiciously.

The pirates looked at each other. These children were asking too many questions. Captain Bumbo edged closer to the treasure chest. He signaled to Mizzy, who began to sing:

*"On the high seas, there's treasure to seize.
Keep close to your ark or be lunch for a shark!"*

The children laughed. "May we use that in our reports?" they asked.

"Of course!" Captain Bumbo said, inching towards the chest. But Mizzy tightened her fists.

"It's my song, Captain!" said Mizzy angrily. "Made from me own brain."

"We can give Mizzy credit," said one of the boys, "you know—write her name in our bibliography at the end of our report."

Mizzy's face lit up, even though she had no idea what a bibliography was.

Just then, Fluke returned. He was carrying the biggest book the captain had ever seen.

"What's that, a book of treasure maps?" Captain Bumbo asked hopefully.

"Hardly, sir," replied Fluke. "It's a dictionary."

"What's a dictionary for? And where's that brain trust of a bird?"

"Don't know about the bird, sir, but a dictionary gives us information about words. It says here that plagiarism is stealing another person's work and pretending it's yours."

"Stealing, aye?" Captain Bumbo grinned from ear to half-ear.

"Hear that, me mateys? We're the Pirates of Plagiarism!"

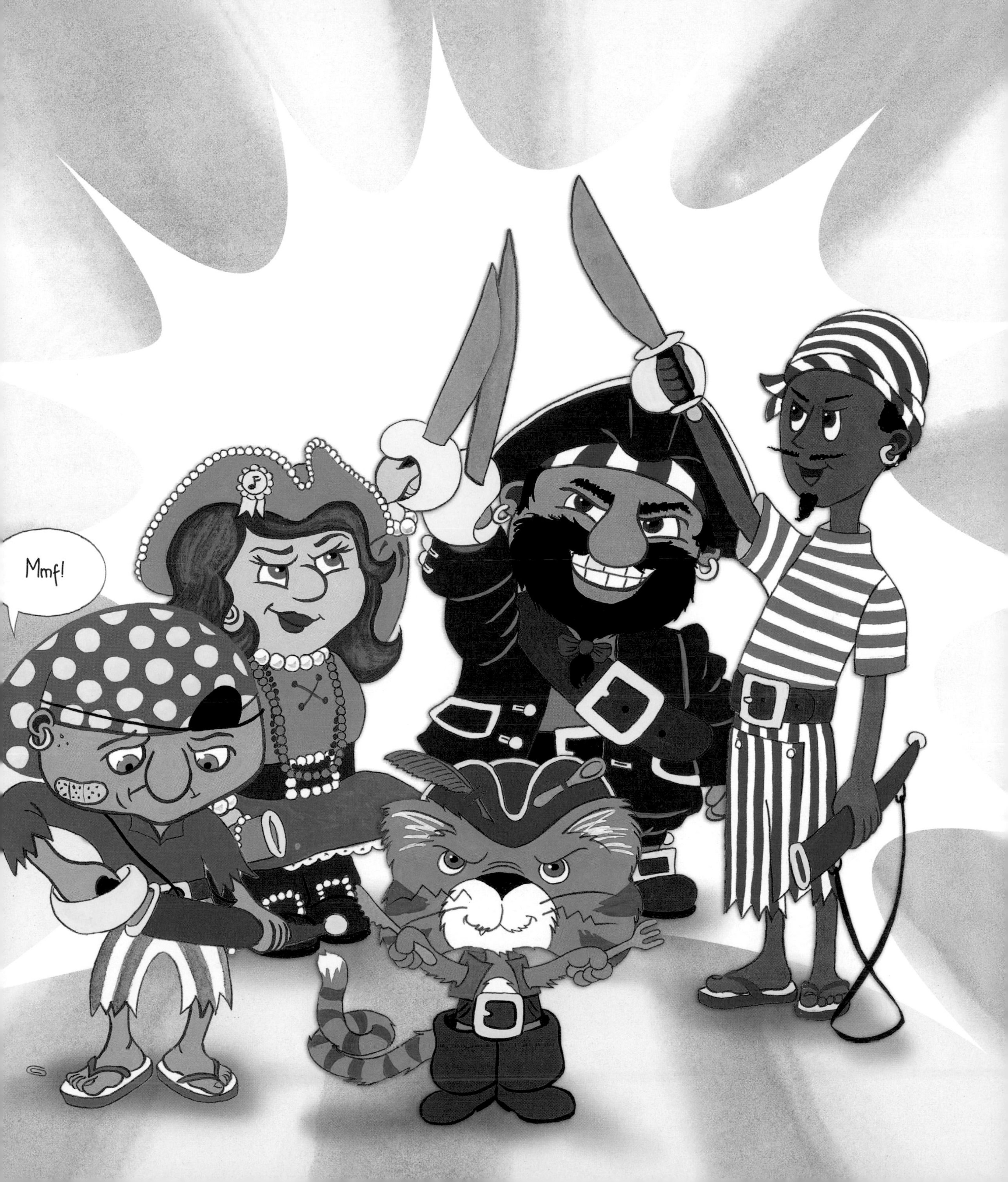

"Quick, mates, grab the loot!" yelled Captain Bumbo. The pirates raced to the treasure chest, hoisted it up, and scurried out the door.

Mrs. Finch and the children ran to the window and watched the Pirates of Plagiarism scramble over the hill.

"When do you think they'll figure out that the chest is empty?" asked a girl.

"They'll find out soon enough," said Mrs. Finch. "The question is, will they ever learn that real treasure can only be found . . ."

"In your brain—RAAWK!—in your brain!"

Plagiarism Dos and Don'ts

DO follow these rules and you may find buried treasure!

- Make a bibliography at the end of your report that says where you found all your information.

- Create artwork that is truly yours and not copied.

- Use quotation marks to mark quotes.

- Document websites where you found ideas.

- Write down where a picture, illustration, or graph in your report came from.

- Write your own stories with your own ideas.

- Take information from the Internet and summarize it in your own words.

- Keep track of all magazines, newspapers, websites, songs, films, and books you use in a school project.

- Give credit to authors and artists whose work you used.

- Use ideas from your own brain.

- Prevent others from plagiarizing your work.

DON'T DO the following, or you'll walk the plank!

- Copy a poem or other text that is not your own work and pretend that it is.

- Put someone else's ideas in your story and say you made them up.

- Use people's words and speeches without quoting them.

- Include a printed picture from the Internet in a report, but not say where you found it.

- Copy word-for-word from an encyclopedia and pretend the words are yours.

- Cheat the real author out of credit for his or her work.

- Let others believe that you created original artwork that you really just traced or copied.

- Steal another person's ideas to get a better grade on a school report.

- Cut and paste ideas from a website into your report without saying you found them online.

- Write a play and take dialogue from another playwright's work.

- Retype a friend's report and hand it in as your own.

- Take a sibling's old book report, add a few new sentences, and turn it in as yours.

To school librarians.
—K. F.

For Tristan, Hannah, Cadence, and Madison
—L. D.

Published by UpstartBooks
4810 Forest Run Road
Madison, WI 53704
1-800-448-4887

The paper used in this publication meets the minimum requirements